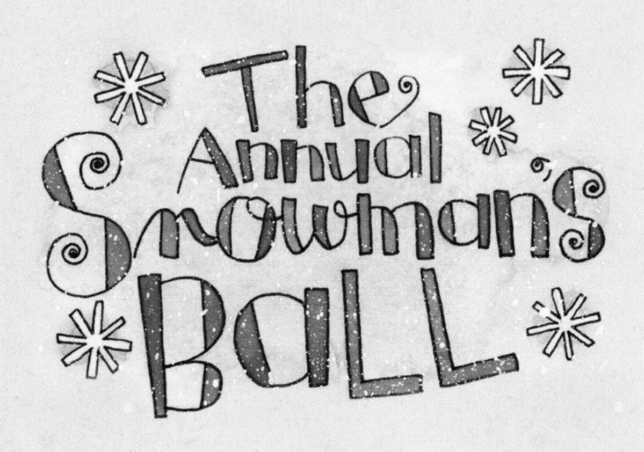
The Annual Snowman's Ball

ISBN-13: 978-0-8249-5564-9

Published by Ideals Children's Books
An imprint of Ideals Publications
A Guideposts Company
535 Metroplex Drive, Suite 250
Nashville, Tennessee 37211
www.idealsbooks.com

Color separations by Precision Color Graphics, Franklin, Wisconsin
Printed and bound in Italy by LEGO

Library of Congress Cataloging-in-Publication Data

Moulton, Mark Kimball.
The annual Snowman's Ball / written by Mark Kimball Moulton ; illustrated by Karen Hillard Good.
p. cm.
Summary: One magical snowy night, Snowman Bob, Snowgirl Sue, and all their friends gather for their annual celebration, with snowball fights, skating, a string orchestra, and delicious food and drink.
ISBN 978-0-8249-5564-9 (alk. paper)
[1. Snowmen--Fiction. 2. Parties--Fiction. 3. Winter--Fiction. 4. Stories in rhyme.] I. Good, Karen Hillard, ill. II. Title.
PZ8.3.M8622An 2007
[E]--dc22
2007005429

10 9 8 7 6 5 4 3 2

Designed by Marisa Jackson

For my beautiful godchildren, Queenie, and everyone who believes in dancing snowmen, talking scarecrows, and everyday angels. —MKM

I would like to dedicate this book to my glorious grandsons, Logan and Lee Thomas (may you have at least three snow days every year!), and my friend Mark for another wonderful story to illustrate! —Karen

The Annual Snowman's Ball

written by
Mark Kimball Moulton

illustrated by
Karen Hillard Good

ideals children's books.
Nashville, Tennessee

I was gazing out my window late one snowy winter's eve,
when from a distance came a sight my eyes could not believe.

For out beyond my backyard, silhouetted by the sky,
I thought I saw a snowman nonchalantly gliding by.

He looked my way and nodded as he cordially tipped his hat,
then smiled before he disappeared just like the Cheshire Cat.

I knew this was impossible—snowmen are made of snow!
They have no feet, and if they did, where would a snowman go?

I ran out on my back porch where I watched another one
slide straight across my back lawn like the other one had done.

And then another snowman and another rolled on by.
My mind was filled with questions—
how could snowmen slide and why?

But what a magic moment,
what a marvel,
what a sight,
to watch a hundred snowmen glide across a moonlit night!

And then a most familiar snowman rolled right up to me.
He bowed and waved and smiled a smile, as friendly as can be.

He wore a black tuxedo with a pocket watch and fob.
Why, I could hardly recognize my Snowman Named Just Bob!

"Wow, Bob!" I cried. "You look so nice in all your fancy clothes."
"Why, thank you. It's a special night as everybody knows.

"The moon is full, the stars are out,
the snow's begun to fall.
Yes, everything is ready for
the Annual Snowman's Ball.

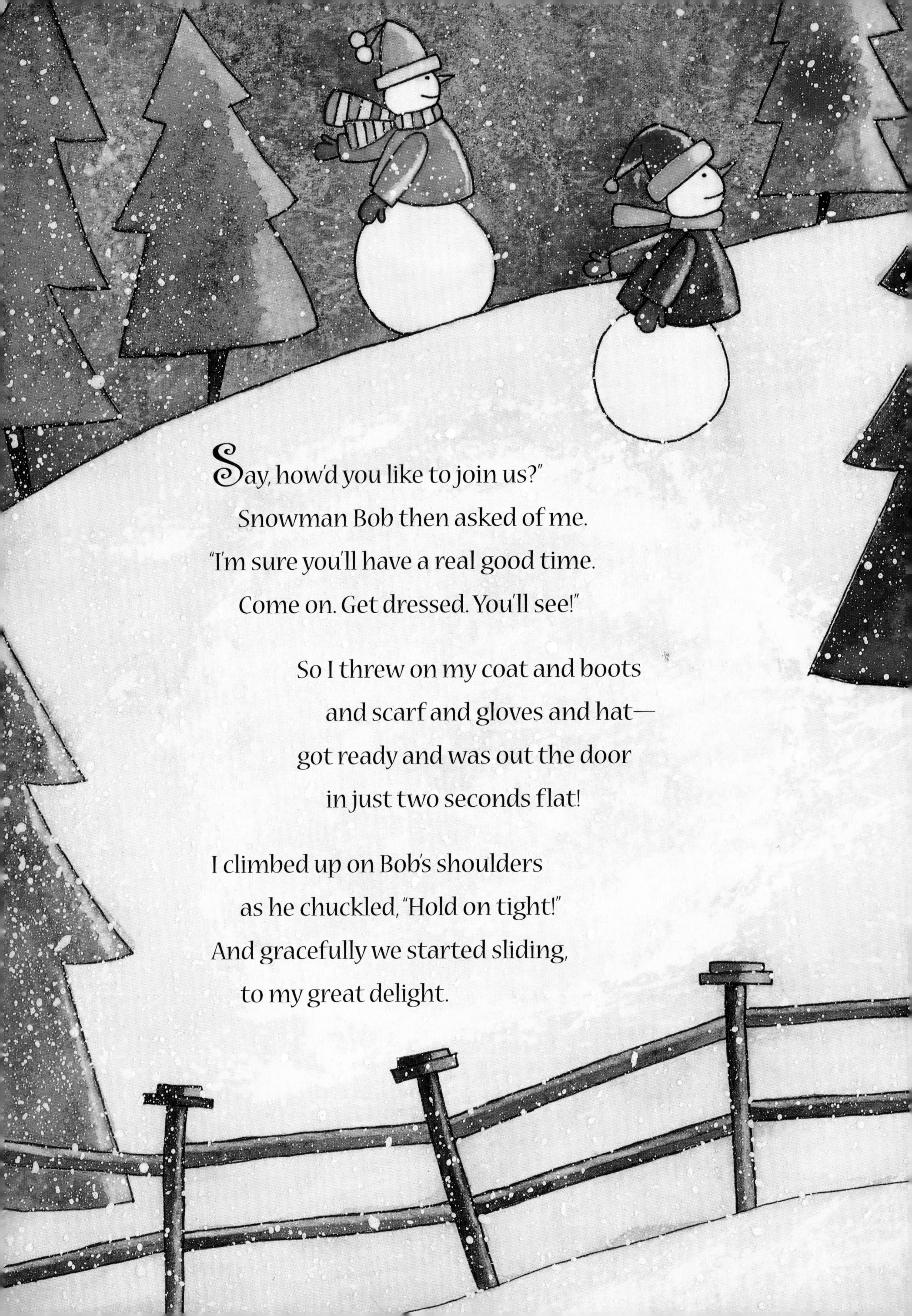

"Say, how'd you like to join us?"
Snowman Bob then asked of me.
"I'm sure you'll have a real good time.
Come on. Get dressed. You'll see!"

So I threw on my coat and boots
and scarf and gloves and hat—
got ready and was out the door
in just two seconds flat!

I climbed up on Bob's shoulders
as he chuckled, "Hold on tight!"
And gracefully we started sliding,
to my great delight.

It was like a secret garden of the richly wooded kind—
the type folks often dream about but very rarely find.

Tall evergreens and stately oaks stood guard around the rim,
all lightly frosted by the snow that clung to every limb.

Brightly colored songbirds sang and flitted here and there,
while mice, raccoons, and chipmunks played
with deer and moose and bear.

Over on the far side was
a frozen skating pond,
and children made of snow were playing
hopscotch just beyond.

Snowmen and snow-ladies stood around a roaring fire,
companionably chatting, dressed in all their best attire.

The bonfire popped and crackled, and it lent a rosy glow
to all the friendly faces of the folks made out of snow.

"But Bob," I cried, "aren't you afraid your friends will melt away?"
"Nope, not at all," he answered me. "At least not on this day!

"You see," he winked, "one night each year a miracle takes place
that puts a happy smile on every cheery snowman's face.

"We laugh and sing and dance and skate
with no concerns at all,
to celebrate the gift of life at this,
our Snowman's Ball!

It really is spectacular. Most everyone attends.
Come on. I'll introduce you now to all my snowman friends."

He took my hand and led me toward a jolly-looking group
who were busy warming up a batch of homemade chicken soup.

Their soup was hot and hit the spot—those snow-folk sure could cook.
We joked and laughed, and when we did, their snow-white bellies shook!

Another group was busy carving hot dog–roasting sticks.
They held them up for me to see and let me have my pick.

Bob took me 'round to everyone, and everyone was nice;
I'd never met so many folks made out of snow and ice!

Some were skinny, some were plump, and some were just plain fat,
with names like Marty, Lee Ann, Peg, and several named just Pat.

Snowgirl Sue then joined us, and Bob kissed her on the cheek.
She blushed, so sweet and cute and shy
that she could hardly speak.

And then she offered me her hand and said,
"I'm glad you came.
I wonder if you'd like to join us in
a snowman game?"

"I've never played a snowman game,
but yes, I think I might."
"Oh, good," she coyly said to me.
"Let's have a snowball fight!"

And with her other hand that she'd kept hidden out of view,
she brought a great big snowball which she aimed at me and threw.

Splaaat! It landed on my coat and took me by surprise.
She giggled and a spark of mischief twinkled in her eyes.

“Why you.” I laughed and bent to make my own big, fluffy ball,

and suddenly a snowball fight broke out, enjoyed by all!

Snowballs zinged and zanged and zipped and zapped around the glade.

Splisht! Splaaat! Swoosh! Swish!

What happy sounds they made!

We laughed until our stomachs hurt,
and when the game was done,
we skated on the frozen pond and had a lot more fun!

The snow fell soft and dreamlike
on the roly-poly skaters,
as plates of food were passed around
by plump, tuxedoed waiters.

There were soup and roasted hot dogs
and warm, gooey s'mores to savor,
and triple-decker snow cones
drenched in tantalizing flavors!

We sat on picnic blankets that
were spread around the glade
and ate up every scrumptious bite
those jolly snow-cooks made.

Then on the breeze I heard
the most romantic, swaying tune,
and suddenly an orchestra was lit up by the moon!

They must have snuck in quietly
and set up unannounced.
The crowd of snowmen clapped and cheered
and whistled, jumped, and bounced.

For this was what they'd waited for.
The ball could now begin!
The snow-folk started dancing,
wearing great big, silly grins.

They waltzed and tangoed gracefully
across the snow-swept floor,
their mouths and fingers sticky from
the ooey, gooey s'mores.

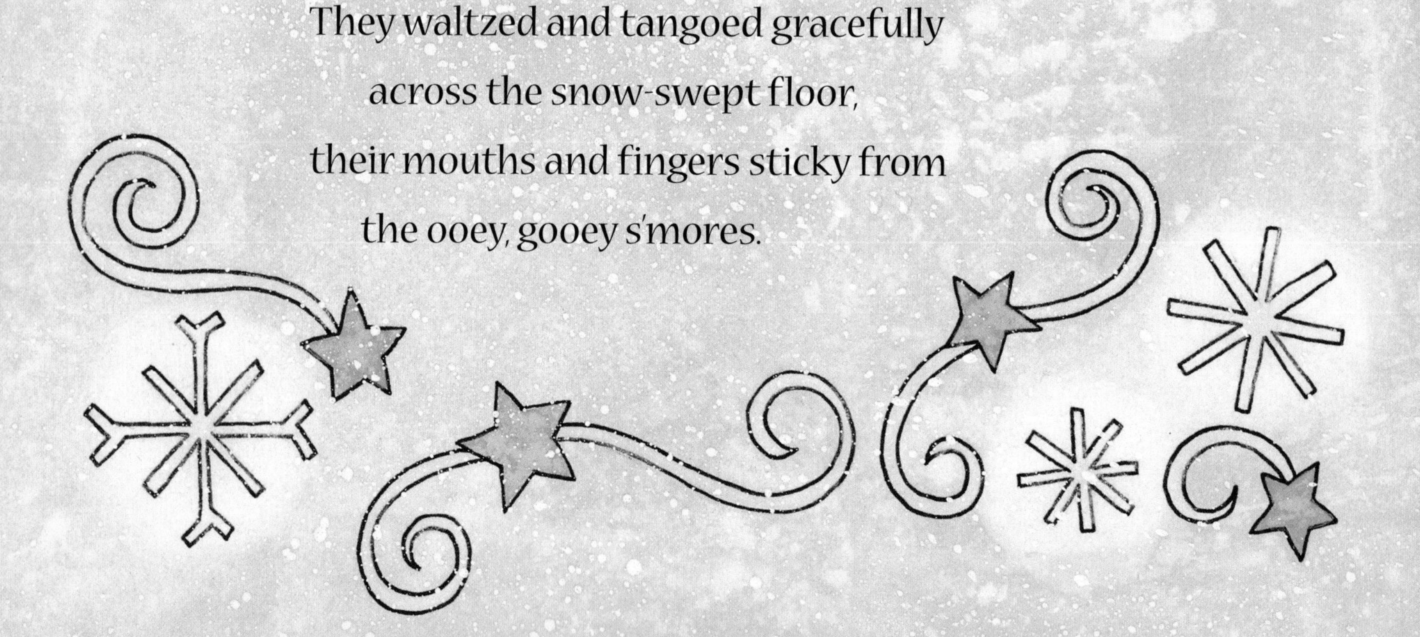

Bob and Sue approached me, and they
asked me for a dance.
I nodded yes emphatically,
excited by the chance.

We held onto each other's hands
as we spun 'round and 'round,
sending little whirlwinds spinning
off the frozen ground.

The snow swirled like the dancers
around Bob and Sue and me—
faster, thicker, heavier
'til I could barely see.

And then I thought I heard my Bob
and his wife named just Sue
call quietly, "Sweet dreams, my friend.
We'll always be with you!"

My eyes grew tired and sleepy. It grew darker overhead.
And then before I knew it, I awoke in my own bed!

"Had there been a Snowman's Ball?" I wondered. "Was it true?
And did I really dance with Snowman Bob and his wife, Sue?"

I ran outside to where my Snowman Bob and Sue both stood,
but they just looked like any other plain old snowmen would.

Instead of being all dressed up, Bob wore his same old coat,
and Sue still wore her mop of hair and scarf around her throat.

I hung my head and turned to leave, and that was when I think...

I saw my Snowman Named Just Bob
give me little wink.

The End